Ohio Dominican College
1216 Sunbury Road
Columbus, Ohio 43219

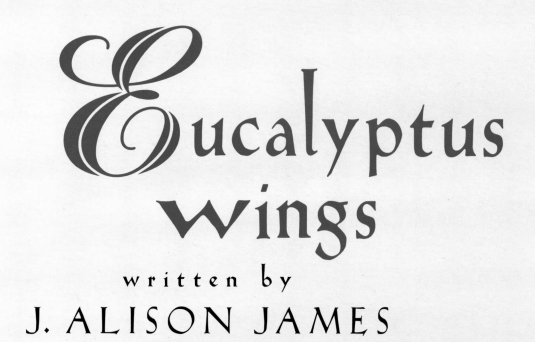

Eucalyptus wings

written by
J. ALISON JAMES

with paintings by
DEMI

ATHENEUM BOOKS FOR YOUNG READERS

Thanks to Ric Peigler
at the Denver Museum of Natural History
for his generous assistance
with finding a moth that pupates on eucalyptus.
And thanks to the Vermont blizzard
that brought Demi and Alison James together.

Atheneum Books for Young Readers
An imprint of Simon & Schuster Children's Publishing Division
1230 Avenue of the Americas
New York, New York 10020
Designed by Ann Bobco
The text of this book is set in Leawood
The illustrations were done in ink and watercolor
Manufactured in Hong Kong
by South China Printing Company (1988) Limited
10 9 8 7 6 5 4 3 2 1

Library of Congress Cataloging-in-Publication Data
James, J. Alison.
Eucalyptus wings / by J. Alison James ; paintings by Demi.
p.   cm.
Summary: Two girls, Kiria and Mica, discover night magic
when Kiria finds a large cocoon suspended from a eucalyptus leaf.
ISBN 0-689-31886-3
[1. Cocoons—Fiction. 2. Magic—Fiction. 3. Flight—Fiction.]
I. Demi, ill. II. Title.
PZ7.J15412Eu   1995
[E]—dc20   95-2130
CIP
AC

For my Papa.
Thanks for the swing, and all the pushes!
—J. A. J.

To living Buddha Lian Seng, who has flown beyond.
—Demi

The wind blew off the sea and swept up the side of Tarahena Mountain like dust from her father's broom. Kiria held her arms out to the wind. Up here, she was higher than the giant eucalyptus tree that grew behind her house and towered over the town below.

Kiria watched the thin silver-blue eucalyptus leaves spin in the wind. "I would fly like those leaves if I could," she said.

Just then, a single leaf flew past, turning with an unbalanced weight. Kiria caught it by the stem. On the underside of the leaf was a cocoon. A long cocoon. Longer than her hand with fingers outstretched.

As she held it, Kiria felt lightning sparkle up her arms.
"Yes!" she whispered. It was magic! Flying magic.

Her feet sprayed stones as she sprinted down the hill.
She ran next door to Mica's house. Mica would know about
magic.

Mica showed the cocoon to her mother.

"Incredible!" Mica's mother said. "I've never seen anything like it."

"I think it's flying magic," Kiria said to Mica.

"It's got to be."

"Magic doesn't just happen,"
Mica said. "You have to do the right
things to get it started." So they
went to the kitchen where they found
the ingredients for a mysterious potion.

Kiria called her father.
"May I spend the night?"
"All right," he said, "But
come home straight away in
the morning. I've got something
to show you."

"All we need now are flying words," Mica said that night in bed.

"Words that fly should be light," said Kiria.

"Like sparkle or dapple . . ." suggested Mica.

"Or flicker . . . " said Kiria. "Wait! I've got it:

Sparkle, dapple, flicker, fly—
Take us sailing through the sky!"

They fell asleep remembering the words.

Deep in the night the moon reached in and shook the curtain.
Kiria woke up.

"Mica," she called softly. "It's time to go. It's time."

They could hear the whispers of the eucalyptus leaves as they
walked through the night up Tarahena. They sprinkled the potion,
held the cocoon, and chanted the words with their eyes closed tight.

"Sparkle, dapple, flicker, fly—
Take us sailing through the sky!"

A warm ribbon of air curled around and lifted them high. . .

until they landed, giggling and tangled in Mica's bed.

They talked until morning of the things they had seen. But when the early sun came sauntering in the open window, they realized what was missing.

The bottle of potion was empty. The cocoon was gone.

"It's over," Kiria said, dismayed. "Now we'll never ever fly again." With the magic gone, even the room felt different, ordinary. "I'd better just go home," she said.

"I'll walk you back, then," said Mica.

Kiria's father was already up and working out back.

"Good morning, girls," he said. "I'm glad you came over early. Come and take a look at what I've made!"

"A swing with ropes so long it'll give you wings.

Get on, and hold tight!"

Then they flew.

Again . . . and again . . .

and again!

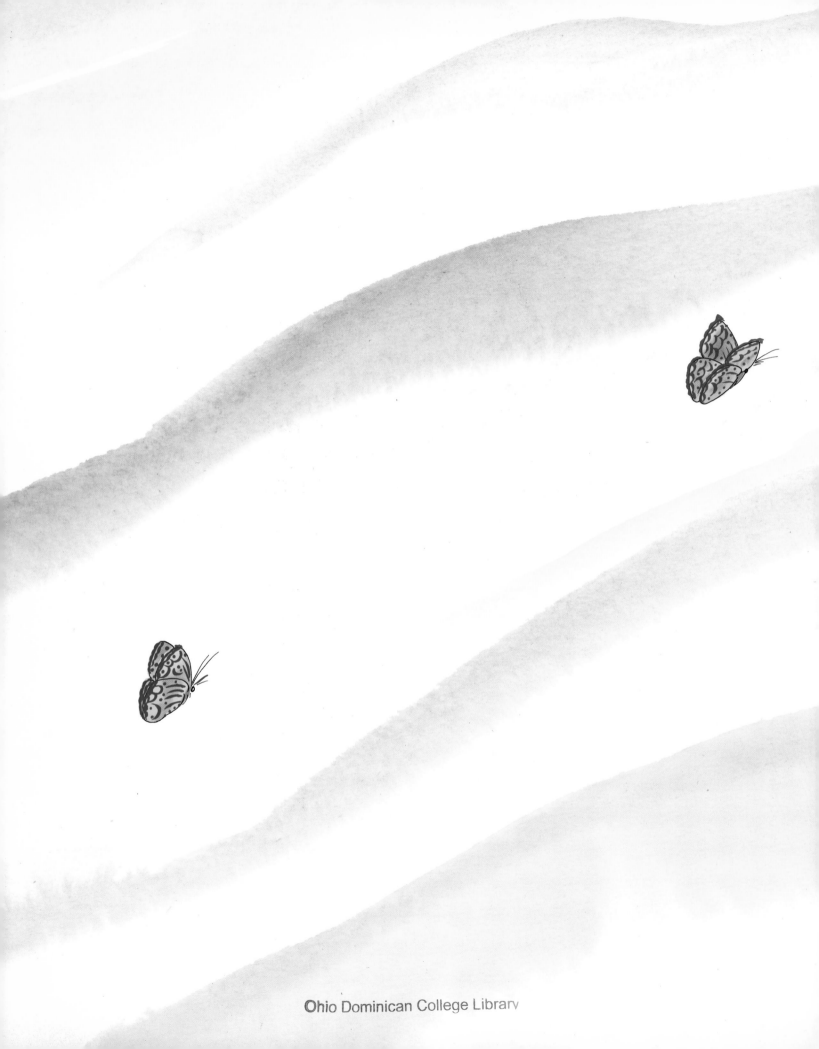